STAR TREK
DEEP SPACE

The Ferengi Rules of Acquisition

By Quark
as told to
Ira Steven Behr

POCKET BOOKS

New York London Toronto Sydney

This book is a work of fiction. Names, characters, places and incidents are
products of the author's imagination or are used fictitiously. Any resemblance
to actual events or locales or persons, living or dead, is entirely coincidental.

An Original Publication of POCKET BOOKS

POCKET BOOKS, a division of Simon and Schuster Inc.
1230 Avenue of the Americas, New York, NY 10020

Copyright © 1995 by Paramount Pictures. All Rights Reserved.

For information about special discounts for bulk purchases,
please contact Simon & Schuster Special Sales: 1-800-456-6798
or business@simonandschuster.com

STAR TREK is a Registered Trademark of
Paramount Pictures.

A VIACOM COMPANY

This book is published by Pocket Books, a division of Simon & Schuster Inc., under
exclusive license from Paramount Pictures.

All rights reserved, including the right to reproduce this book or portions thereof in
any form whatsoever. For information address Pocket Books, 1230 Avenue of the
Americas, New York, NY 10020

ISBN: 978-0-671-52936-9

First Pocket Books trade paperback printing July 1995

10 9

POCKET and colophon are registered trademarks of
Simon & Schuster Inc.

Cover design by Steve Ferlauto; cover photo by Tom Zimberoff

ACKNOWLEDGMENTS

Ira Steven Behr would like to thank the following people for their help with both the Rules of Acquisition and this book: Rick Berman, Michael Piller, Peter Allan Fields, James Crocker, Ronald D. Moore, Rene Echevarria, Evan Carlos Somers, David S. Cohen & Martin A. Winer, Sheri Lynn Behr, Michael & Denise Okuda, Robbin Slocum, Nell Crawford, Lolita Fatjo, Bob Gillan, John Ordover, Rick Schultz, and especially Robert Hewitt Wolfe, who knows these Rules as well as I do, and my wife, Laura Behr, who kept telling me "write the book, write the book."

Quark would like to thank Armin Shimerman, for reasons of a personal nature.

A FEW WORDS
FROM QUARK

Congratulations. I'm proud of you. You've made a wise purchase. The book you hold in your hands represents the sum total of Ferengi business wisdom. All right, maybe not the sum total. I suppose if you want to be technical what you're holding in your hands represents approximately one-quarter of the sum total of Ferengi business wisdom. If you're wondering how I reached that figure, it's really quite simple. You see, there are two hundred and eighty-five Rules of Acquisition. This book contains seventy—or about one-quarter of the total Rules. But believe me when I tell you, one-quarter of the sum total of Ferengi business

v

wisdom is still a lot of wisdom. I doubt you humans could handle much more.

Now, I know what some of you are thinking. Just what *are* the Ferengi Rules of Acquisition? Good question. So for those of you who bought this book on the strength of the cover alone (and yes, that is your humble author standing there—have you ever seen such a devastating smile, such photogenic lobes?), I'd be happy to explain. The Rules of Acquisition consist of the two hundred and eighty-five guiding principles that form the basis of Ferengi business philosophy. A philosophy that has enabled the Ferengi people to become the most successful entrepreneurs in the galaxy. Think about it. Don't you want to increase your earning potential? Don't you want to make bigger, more lucrative business deals? Don't you want to double, triple, maybe even quadruple your profits?

I know I do.

And you do too.

Well then, this book is for you. Now, about these Rules . . .

Hold on!

YOU.

That's right, you! The one standing hunched over in that bookstore aisle reading this book. Stop! You heard me. I know what you're up to. You think you can read this entire book straight through, right there in that bookstore, then return it to the shelves and walk away having learned all its secrets WITHOUT COMPENSATING ITS AUTHOR. Well, I've got news for you, my friend: that's not how it works. Now, before you read another sentence I want you to close this book, carry it over to the salesperson ... AND PAY FOR IT. And while you're at it buy some copies for your friends. And your family. And any business colleagues you may have. Believe me, they need to own this book just as much as you do. So go ahead, buy a lot of copies. They'll thank you for it. And so will I.

Now don't let the slender size of this volume fool you. *The Ferengi Rules of Acquisition* is definitely *not* a book that can be read once and then tossed aside. Not if you truly want to profit from its lessons. No, the Rules are meant to be studied, weighed, evaluated, contemplated, mulled over, and reflected on until each word has been absorbed into your memory. In fact, I'd go so far as to say that *The Ferengi Rules of Acquisition* is the only book you need to own. Well, maybe not the only book. I'd also suggest you get yourself a copy of *The Ferengi Guide to Sexual Fulfillment: The Joys of Oo-moxing*. Anyone interested in purchasing a copy can do so by sending three strips of gold-pressed latinum to:

QUARK
c/o *Deep Space Nine*
Bajor Sector
Alpha Quadrant*

But to get back to the Rules. Don't let their simplicity fool you. Ferengi business scholars have been interpreting and debating them for thousands of years—ever since the first Grand Nagus, the gloriously devious Gint himself, wrote those immortal words, "Even in the

---

*Please allow six to eight weeks for delivery.

viii

worst of times, someone turns a profit." Although that was, in fact, the first Rule of Acquisition ever committed to parchment, Gint, in a shrewd marketing ploy, labeled it the One Hundred and Sixty-Second Rule. Why? To increase the demand for the first one hundred and sixty-one. That Gint, always thinking.

Now, the way I see it, you have two choices. One is to carry this book with you at all times. That way, if you find yourself in the middle of a business negotiation, and you're not sure what your next move should be, you can whip out your copy of the Rules and thumb through it until you find an appropriate solution. Personally, I find this choice to be both lazy and inefficient. Your second choice is to do what I do. To do what all Ferengi do. Memorize the entire book. Okay, okay, I know that sounds a little daunting at first. But is it really?! I don't think so. All it takes is to memorize one Rule a day. That's not so bad when you think about it. In less than a year I was able to memorize all two hundred and eighty-five Rules. And you only have to memorize seventy. So the point is, if you want the Rules to work for you, you have to work on the Rules.

I know what you're thinking. Is it worth it? Will memorizing seventy Rules of Acquisition really make a difference in your life? Boy, you humans ask some pretty stupid questions. Of course it will make a difference. Aren't you tired of watching someone else make all the profit? Don't you wish you lived in a big house, had expensive possessions, went on fun-filled vacations? Of course you do. We all do. Well, here's your chance.

Look, don't be shy. Why don't you say what's really on your mind. After all, we're friends, aren't we? All right, I'll say it for you: "So far, Quark's made a lot of promises. How do I know I can trust him?" In other words, you want a guarantee that the Ferengi Rules of Acquisition will do everything I've said they will. Make you wealthier. Make you smarter. Make you more appealing. Don't worry. I'm not offended. It only makes me realize how desperately you need to learn these Rules. You want a guarantee? You need a guarantee? First turn to Rule Number Nineteen.

x

Go ahead.

I'll wait.

There, does that answer your question? Well, guarantee or no guarantee, the only thing you have to ask yourself is what do you have to lose? If the answer is nothing—and what other answer is there?—then you've got some reading to do. but before I send you off to get the most important education of your life, there's one last thing you should know. Ever since I decided to compile this book, my brother Rom has wondered why. Why am I doing it? Why am I willing to share the secrets of Ferengi success with a bunch of undeserving humans? Is it just to earn some extra profit? Is it to promote a better understanding between humans and Ferengi? Or is it to show an inferior race just how superior we Ferengi are?

The answer is none of the above.

The reason this book exists is because I have a dream. A dream of a brighter future that I firmly believe will change my life forever. A dream that will bring me greater profit than I've ever imagined. A dream that I am determined to turn into the greatest single business deal of my career. And that dream can be summed up in seven little words:

Quark's Ferengi Rules of Acquisition—
The Movie.

Once you have their money . . . you never give it back.

2

Never pay more
for an acquisition
than you have to.

Never allow
family to stand in the
way of opportunity.

#7

Keep your ears open.

Small print leads
to large risk.

Opportunity plus instinct equals profit.

Greed is eternal.

8

#13

Anything worth
doing is worth
doing for money.

A deal is a deal
... until a better
one comes along.

#18

A Ferengi
without profit is no
Ferengi at all.

Satisfaction is not guaranteed.

N ever place
friendship above
profit.

14

#22

A wise man can hear profit in the wind.

15

There's nothing more dangerous than an honest businessman.

#31

Never make fun
of a Ferengi's
mother ... insult
something he cares
about instead.

#33

It never hurts to
suck up to the
boss.

18

Peace is good for business.

#35

War is good for business.

She can touch
your lobes but
never your latinum.

Profit is its own reward.

24

Never confuse
wisdom with luck.

Don't trust
a man wearing
a better suit than
your own.

#48

The bigger the smile, the sharper the knife.

Never ask when you can take.

Good customers
are as rare as
latinum—treasure
them.

There is no
substitute for success.

#59

Free advice is
seldom cheap.

31

#60

Keep your lies consistent.

33

The riskier the
road, the greater
the profit.

Win or lose,
there's always
Huyperian beetle
snuff.

Home is where the heart is . . . but the stars are made of latinum.

Every once in a
while, declare
peace. It confuses
the hell out of your
enemies.

#79

Beware of the
Vulcan greed for
knowledge.

41

The flimsier the product, the higher the price.

#85

Never let the competition know what you're thinking.

43

Ask not what your profits can do for you, but what you can do for your profits.

Females and
finances don't mix.

Enough . . . is never enough.

Trust is the
biggest liability
of all.

48

#102

Nature decays,
but latinum lasts
forever.

Faith moves mountains . . . of inventory.

There is no honor
in poverty.

Dignity and an
empty sack is
worth the sack.

Treat people in
your debt like family
... exploit them.

Never have sex
with the boss's
sister.

Always have sex
with the boss.

56

#117

You can't free a
fish from water.

Everything is for sale, even friendship.

Even a blind man
can recognize the
glow of latinum.

Wives serve,
brothers inherit.

#141

O nly fools pay retail.

There's nothing wrong with charity . . . as long as it winds up in *your* pocket.

#162

Even in the worst
of times someone
turns a profit.

Know your
enemies ... but do
business with them
always.

Not even dishonesty can tarnish the shine of profit.

#189

Let others keep
their reputation.
You keep their
money.

#192

Never cheat a Klingon ... unless you're sure you can get away with it.

It's always good
business to know
about new customers
before they walk in
your door.

#202

The justification
for profit is profit.

Never begin a negotiation on an empty stomach.

Always know what you're buying.

#223

Beware the man
who doesn't make
time for *oo-mox*.

Latinum lasts
longer than lust.

#236

You can't buy
fate.

More is good
... all is better.

#255

A wife is a luxury . . . a smart accountant a necessity.

A wealthy man
can afford anything
except a conscience.

#266

When in doubt, lie.

#284

Deep down
everyone's a
Ferengi.

80

#285

No good deed
ever goes
unpunished.

New rules are being revealed to you humans all the time. You can keep track of them here. Don't think this means you won't have to buy a revised and expanded edition of this book someday.

Rule #

_____

Rule #

_____

Rule #

_____

Rule #

_____

Rule #

_____

Rule #

_____

Rule #

_____

Rule #

_____

Rule #

_____

CPSIA information can be obtained
at www.ICGtesting.com
Printed in the USA
LVHW040852030821
694403LV00011B/776

9 780671 529369

CAMILLA

By Camilla Allsop

brightlings.co

Published by Brightlings, 2020

brightlings.co

Chapter 1

One sunny morning in Sydney under the sea a smart little girl named Camilla had a big secret, she is a mermaid that can turn into a human she's never told any one. She woke up and tip-toed past her mean big brother and passed her foolish parents. Camilla went to the Sea Library and she read eight and a half books but she had to leave because her parents would usually wake up at this time and if she got caught she would have to be locked in her room for eight whole hours! Isn't that CRAZY! While we are walking back to Camilla's house I'll tell you facts about her. Camilla loves reading and her wish of all wishes is to be in school. Ok, now where at Camilla's worn down old home, she went to the kitchen and waited only five seconds till her foolish parents, Mr and Mrs Lamwood and her mean big brother named Nico arrived to have breakfast .They all had Nutella pancakes they were delicious but the only thing that was wrong was that they did was they didn't make delicious Nutella pancakes for Camilla sad isn't it? Well I would be sad if I was Camilla Lamwood. One dark night Mr.Lamwood was at work and found a foolish and mean principle called Miss Mia. Do you think you know what's going to happen? Have a guess, well if you really want to know keep reading! The next day while Camilla was reading an adventurous book her dad knocked on Camilla's door and came in. He said " do you want to go to school today?" Camilla obviously said "yes please", "well it's starting in one hour get ready now" Mr Lamwood said in a mad voice!So in an hour she skipped down cheerfully down the path and arrived at her new school. It looked a bit dull.

Chapter 2

When Camilla went into her new school she met a friend called Lily she was crazy,
smart and funny but the mean principle came and her name was Miss Mia. Everyone stood very still but left a pathway for Mrs Mia, but Camilla and Lily hid behind a tall delicate brown wall but a girl called Lulu warned Camilla and Lily if Miss Mia found out that you are standing behind this wall you would get in humongous trouble ! So they tip toed around the wall into the crowd and hoping that nobody sees them they really didn't want Miss Mia to see them otherwise they would get in huge trouble! Normally people would have to eat 100 bugs isn't that crazy but as they tip toed the in front delicate wall three sassy girls Tracy, Macy and Stacey walked by and saw them and told Mrs Mia . One of the sassy girls was Mrs Mia's daughter , Tracy so Tracy did tell on

her and Mrs Mia was very angry at Camilla,Lily and Lulu and they had to eat 100 bugs each it was disgusting! And even one girl got thrown over the fence.But on the bright side me Lily and Lulu are in the same class and their teacher is really beautiful and kind her name is Miss Sarah. Her first lesson was maths and Miss Sarah said " what's 1278 times 3000? and Camilla shouted out 3834000 then Miss Sarah checked on her phone and the answer was correct Miss Sarah was wowed by Camilla's smartness so we're all the classmates.Ding the lunch bell rang!

Chapter 3

Miss Sarah went to Mrs Mia's office and knocked on the door . Knock Knock! Then Miss Mia slammed the door open and said "What do you want!"and Miss Sarah said "well I think Camilla could go up 2 grades , she can multiply big numbers like 3000 times 1278 she's really smart!" " I knew it her father said she was a nit wit and you my daughter can't even stand her!" Shouted Mrs Mia "No it's not like that I love her being teacher " said Miss Sarah " get out said Mrs Mia so Miss Sarah did get out and got ready to teach science. As the bell rang lunch time was over and children ran to there classrooms Camilla's class 2P were learning about light and sound today they made an instrument that could reflect light and change pitch Camilla thought it was very fun!There next lesson was art ! Art was Camilla's favourite subject in school 2P did an echidnas modelled with clay the eye were googly eyes and the spikes were snapped toothpicks it was very prickly !

Ding! The bell for afternoon tea this calls for a delicious snack like chocolate chip cookies! Yummy!

After afternoon tea 2P sang a school song "This is are are school we share it together forever when someone's hurt you help then up care about them and tell a lovely teacher because we are The Institute for naughty children."

Chapter 4

After they sang the song 2P herd a loud kick that was supposed to be a knock. Knock! knock ! It was Mrs Mia the principle The children were all frightened as Mrs Mia yelled " Sit down you nit wits !" "Let's play a little eh it called what's your idea of a perfect school I'll go first.""Now do you know what my idea of a perfect school is?"

" No we do not may you please tell us Mrs Mia " replied 2P

"Well my idea of a perfect school is with no children at all !" said Mrs Mia

" It wouldn't be a school if their wasn't children " said Lily confused

" Don't question me !" Shouted Mrs Mia

"Sorry Mrs Mia." replied Lily

"You go to my office now !" Shouted Mrs Mia

"No," "Please don't send her to your office " Miss Sarah said scaredly.

"You know what I'm leaving" Yelled Mrs Mia and she slammed the door shut. BANG!

"Are you guys alright? " Miss Sarah said kindly as 2P hugged each other scaredly.

A few minutes later it was home time, Camilla had a lot of homework to Complete from Miss Mia

Chapter 5

The next day Camilla went to school was surprisingly the same in the morning isn't that weird? The only thing that was different was that lulu told Camilla that every morning it's the same . Camilla was very confused.

"Miss Mia " wispred Lulu

"You!"" Piggy tale girl!" Shouted Mrs Mia

"Yes Mrs Mia." Said Isabella

"Do we allow pigs at this school"

"No Mrs Mia " Isabella said shyly

"Well then why are you wearing piggy tales" shouted Mrs Mia

"Because my mummy thinks I look cute in piggy tales"said Isabella proudly.

"Your mummy is not here so ask your teacher to take them out this instant I will check at lunch time
 Ok said Isabella

So when she went in her classroom she asked Miss Sarah to undo Isabella's piggy tales and miss Sarah questioned " Why do you have leafs and twigs in your hair?"

"Mrs Mia threw me across the fence over to Allsop Garden."cried Isabella "It hurt" said Isabella crying in pain the 2P had Science then English and then mathematics then it was lunch after lunch 2P had art then they played with robots! Ring! It was afternoon tea

After afternoon tea 2P went to Spanish class with Miss Valeria then after it was home time and miss Sarah asked Camilla if she wants to have a cup of tea at her place and Camilla said "Yes please."
An hour later Camillas family picked her up because they were going to a permanent vacation to Mexico City but Camilla didn't want to leave Sydney so she said " Can Miss Sarah adopt me?"and Mrs Lamwood said we don't have the adoption papers and do you think Miss Mia would like to adopt you

Camilla said "I have the adoption papers in my school bag!" "And I would love to adopt her!"

"Can you guys Sign The papers please!"

" alright alright" Mrs and Mr Lamwood said

"YAY!" shouted Camilla

And how bad things were were how good things became.

One school day everyone threw some of the food at Mrs Mia and she was never heard or seen from again. And Miss Sarah became the principal and Camilla became a teacher because she was so smart! The school is now called school for everyone!

THE END

THE END

CPSIA information can be obtained
at www.ICGtesting.com
Printed in the USA
LVHW040852030821
694403LV00011B/777